# Special Memories

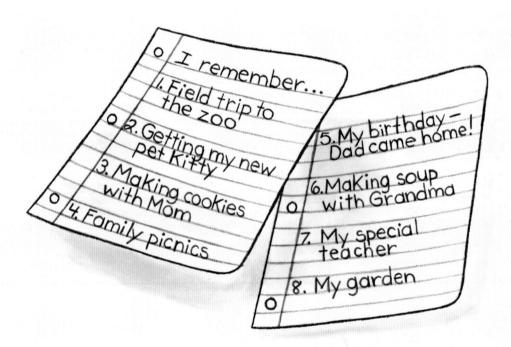

Think of a special memory,
One you won't forget.

Like the time you went to the zoo
Or the day you got your pet.

3

Remember the day you baked cookies
With your mom or with a friend.

4

Remember another special day
You wished would never end.

TEDDY BEAR
ORCHESTRA
ADMIT ONE

NOW YOU
ARE 7!

Grandma's Cookies
3 cups flour
1 cup sugar
½ cup shortening
1 tsp. salt, ½ cup water
Combine. Roll out. Cut.
Bake at 350°
for 10-12 minutes

HAWAII!

Think about your memories.
Don't let them fade away.

Ann's Journal

I love to make cookies with Gram. I love sugar cookies. Gram loves macaroons.

Then **write** about your memories.
Write a little every day.

Remember a special birthday.
Remember the happy times—

8

Making soup with Grandma
And Grandpa's funny rhymes.

9

Think of a family picnic
Or a time with Mom or Dad.

10

Remember when you helped someone
When they were feeling sad.

11

Did you ever have a teacher
Who showed you something new?

Did you ever pick tomatoes
From a garden that you grew?

Things to write about
1. Fishing with Dad.
2. Great Grandpa's railroad watch.
3. My class trip to the museum.
4. Our vacation at the seashore.
5. My bird.

Idea! Spot's birthday

Think about your memories.
Don't let them fade away.

14

I remember
Spot's first
birthday. It
was so fun!

Today, I

Then **write** about your memories.
Write a little every day.

1. Keep a list of special memories in your journal. Write in your journal, a little every day.

2. Help with your family's photo book or scrapbook. Write captions to go with the pictures.

When baby Justin came home, I got to hold him for the first time

This is Grandpa and Grandma meeting baby Justin. Justin has Grandpa's forehead.